Have You Considered the Egg?

Marian Pilgrim

authorHOUSE®

AuthorHouse™ UK
1663 Liberty Drive
Bloomington, IN 47403 USA
www.authorhouse.co.uk
Phone: 0800 047 8203 (Domestic TFN)
+44 1908 723714 (International)

Published by AuthorHouse 05/06/2016

ISBN: 978-1-5246-3392-9 (sc)
ISBN: 978-1-5246-3394-3 (e)

Print information available on the last page.

This book is printed on acid-free paper.

2/11/99

Spiritual Biblical

The Psychology of Christianity in a Practical, Attainable Way

"Christ" -- (1) Love
Share
Give

"Heaven" -- (2)
"Road" -- (3)
"Inspiration" -- (4)
"Spirit" -- (5)
"Truth" -- (6)
"Insight" -- (7)
"Acceptance" -- (8)
"Need" -- (9)
"Individual" -- (10)
"Think" -- (11)
"Yield" -- (12)

The Lord's Prayer

Matthew 6: 9-13

My Father which art in heaven, hallowed be thy name. Thy kingdom come, thy will be done in earth, as it is in heaven. Give me this day my daily bread. And forgive me my debts, as I forgive my debtors. And lead me not into temptation, but deliver me from evil; for thine is the kingdom, and the power, and the glory, forever. Amen.

My father in heaven, blessed be your name. Bring your kingdom and make this earth as your throne. Feed me daily forgive me as I forgive others. Let me not be tempted and keep me from evil for such is your kingdom, power and glory.

17/10/2004

When God created the earth, nature found a solution to the problem of preventing the (eggs) from being crushed by the weight of the hen bird as she sat on the nest to incubate them. The solution was the characteristic egg shape, which provides structural strength, to withstand all-round pressure even with a thin shell. (If the shell were thick, the chick inside would not be able to peck its way out). The eggs have a rounded profile over the whole surface. When you grip an egg, the force you apply is transmitted in all directions away from the point of contact by the curve of the egg. The results is the force being distributed over a wide area, and no exccessive stress being set up at any one point. Such is the Christian life's: "How is it done?" Readers Digest 1st Edition 1990

Contents

1. CHRISTIANITY LOVE 1
2. HEAVEN 6
3. ROAD 9
4. SPIRIT 17
5. TRUST 20
6. What is TRUTH? 25
7. INSIGHT 27
8. ACCEPTANCE 32
9. NEED 34
10. INDIVIDUAL 37
11. THINK 40
12. YIELD 42

11/10/2000

PREFACE

To the S.D.A Church Members.

At the time I wrote these spiritual ideas, I hoped that one day many of my Christian friends would find it a privilege to read and understand this simple, workable psychology, for living.

The dynamic laws which the writing tries to put forward were learned the hard way by trials as a Christian in the pathway of life. I found the sayings true to my own problems and believe me, I know they worked. This is just to share my effort of Spiritual Psychology to others, for if it helped me, I felt it might also be of help to others.

In formulating this simple psychology of life, I found my own answers from the bible. The scriptures merely describe those truths in language and thought forms understandable to us today and in the New Millinium. The way of the Christian life as written is very wonderful. It is not easy, indeed, it often is hard, but it is full of joy and hope and victory.

I can remember when I sat to write, the only ability that I possessed came from the inspiration of God's words. So I had an earnest prayer session asking for guidance while putting the entire work in the hands of God.

I asked only that this might help people to live more effective lives. "It teaches the cultivation of peace of mind, not as an escape from life into protected quiescence, but as a power center out of which comes driving energy for constructive psychological living. It teaches positive thinking not as a means to fame, riches or power, but as the practical application of faith to overcome defeat and accomplish worthwhile creative values in spiritual living."

May God continue to use these works to bring psychological healing to human helplessness.

INTRODUCTION

These works were written to suggest techniques and give examples which demonstrate that you do not need to be defeated by anything along the Christian pathway. You can have peace of mind and never-ceasing energy flowing forth from the joy and satisfaction spiritual psychology offers. Too often many of us Christians become defeated by everyday problems of life. We go struggling, perhaps even whining through our days with a sense of dull resentment at what we may consider as a "bad break". But there is a spiritual psychological aspect by which we can control and even determine those breaks. We can overcome such attitudes by not allowing ourselves to be defeated by the problems, cares, and difficulties of our human existence. As Christians we cannot permit obstacles to control our mind to the point where they are uppermost and thus become the dominating factor in our thought pattern.

By learning Spiritual Psychology we can cast our mind on spiritual things, refusing to become mentally subservient to them, and channeling spiritual power through our thought which can raise us above the obstacles which ordinarily might defeat us.

The methods I have outlined should help us through the obstacle of Christian living, and as a result new life, new power, increased efficiency, greater happiness and joy will be your days. These works teaches applied spiritual psychology, which is a simple yet scientific system of practical techniques of successful living that works.

17/11/2000

SPIRITUAL Psychology

According to Gary Zukav (1990) "Psychology means soul knowledge. It means the study of the spirit, but it has never been that. Psychology is the study of cognition perceptions and affects. It is the study of the personality."

In order to develop and nurture your mind and your body, it would be of great importance to realise that you have a mind and a body. To be able to heal directly at the level of the soul it is imperitive to acknowledge that everyone has a soul. Thus as Christians we can develop a healthy and disciplined mind, an intellect that can expand wholesomely and fully into any task that requires more than merely recognizing the existence of the mind. How the mind works, what it desires, what strengthens it and what weakens it, and then applying that knowledge is of great importance to the Christian journey here below.

Spiritual Psychology is a new discipline of the spirit that is truly of the spirit, that has its focus on the soul of the human being. The healing power at the Core of Psychology is the power of consciousness. Seeking out, facing with courage, and bringing into the light of consciousness that which is unconsciousness, and therefore, in a position of power over the personality, is what heals. The exploration and understanding of intuition has come to be the central part of Spiritual Psychology. Thus intuition is that voice you hear not with your physical ears, but that connection between your personality and its higher self guided by the spirit. This form of recognition often becomes the focus of one's attention as a curiosity and is often not processed by the intellect.

Spirituality will be at the core of spiritual psychology. Therefore spiritual psychology will be oriented towards spirituality and spiritual crises will be considered legitimate sufferings. Thus spirituality has to do with the immortal process itself. "You have your intuitions, for example, but your spirituality is not limited to your personality and its intuitional system. Your spirituality encompasses your whole soul's journey, whereas your intuition is the way that your soul can contact your beingness to help it in survival situations, or in creative situations, or in inspirational situations." It is the means through which you can pray to God and ask for help and guidance. Spiritual psychology is a disciplined and systematic study of what is necessary to the health of the soul. Spiritual psychology will bring to light those situations that would shatter the spirit if seen clearly. So the soul cannot tolerate jealousies, hatreds, anger or being lied to. These behaviours distort and contaminate and destroy the strength of the soul.

Understanding this dynamic is at the heart of spiritual psychology. It is the foundation upon which spiritual psychology is built so that when ??? is seen it is not responded to with judgement or ugliness or avoidance, but recognised as the shattered soul. Spiritual Psychology addresses this situation by addressing directly the issue of authentic power. Spiritual Psychology will support the choice to learn through wisdom, the choice to release negative influences such as anger, doubt and fear. Thus our relationship between the personality and the soul will become clear. We will be able to see the differences between them and recognize those differences.

CHRISTIANITY
LOVE

I

Psychologists would probably have been wise to have abdicated responsibility for analysis of this term and left it to poets.

The confusing litter left behind by lack of wisdom and excess of boldness can, however, be codifine by the following classification scheme. First, the two most general uses of the term: (a) An intense feeling of strong liking or affection for some specific person/persons. (b) An enduring sentiment towards a person producing a desire to be with that person and a concern for the happiness and satisfactions of that person. Note that both of these may or may not carry sexual connotation. The primary role played by love in either of these senses is that it is an effective state that is assumed to color all interactions with and perceptions of the person loved. It is this component, of course, that makes love so attractive to psychologists.)

Z. RUBIN SCALE which evaluate 3 components (1) affiliative/dependent needs. (2) predisposition to help. (3) exclusiveness.

? Is love innate or is it an acquire emotional response?
? Can the feeling of love be dissociated from the behaviour or does the emotion always contaminate ???

1 Corinthians 13 1-13 speaks of love that is innate yet have an emotional response. Thus if a person do much talking and do not have love there is an emptiness within and a void without.

There are folks who are capable of understanding great scientific knowledge, but without love from within their souls, achieve nothing with their academic skills. You see some people go about showing emotional responses by feeding the unfortunate people. Some stand up for social injustices, but when such love is shown it can be the dissociated from the person's behaviour or the person's emotion response becoming contaminated by their actions.

Innate love is long lasting, kind, does not envy others, neither puts the persons thoughts to think that they are better than another person or people. Thus they do not act in a puffed up manner. To understand that this love is from within the person do not act stupid by doing his or her own thing and becoming angry when others tell them so. Thus they would not think of doing evil when rebuked.

The person with an innate love don't get their joys from the wrongs of others but becomes glad when truth is told. They are able to handle whatever comes their way believing the things they hear while hoping them to be true. Their endurance is strong.

Innate love never ends, but the external will dissapear. We know that context theory -(A theoretical point of view maintaining that all behaviour must be analyzed within the context in which it occurs, that to interpret any act independently of context will ultimately be misleading.) When the person leaves childhood and become an adult love which was innate either grows or can become emotional responses acquired from external forces.

Revelation 2:17 speaks of the new name written on a white stone, which no one knoweth but he that receiveth it, surely suggests how individual and secret and, in a sense, incommunicable is the experience of God within each believer's heart. Is this new and secret name a name by which God Himself is made known to the soul? If so, it suggests that God discloses Himself in some unique and personal way to each faithful heart. My personality is different from that of my brother; therefore God will not come to me just as He comes to him. Each of us sees God from his own angle, finds in God the completion of his own distinctive life, the answer to his own solitary need. So I may come to have my own name for God, a name that for my weakness is a strong tower, for my weariness a fountain of joy and refreshing. It may be that I must wrestle through long hours of darkness before I come to know the name by which henceforth I shall call Him. But when once God has told His name to me, life can never be the same again. Henceforth I carry the secret knowledge in my heart, this name that stands for what God is to me, for what I have found and am finding still in Him. Or is this new and secret name a name which God Himself bestows upon the believing soul? Is it, not my name for God, but His name for me? If so, here is a gracious suggestion of the tenderness, the intimacy of God's ways with the soul. He has his own name for each of His children. Just as-and we need not shrink from such a comparison; All Scripture encourages us to see in our human loves the shadow of the divine – just as lovers have their own tender names for one another, their own secret language of affection and delight, so God and the soul have their own secret communications their own intimate names. The name by which God calls me may be the name of something that He alone sees in me. It may be the name of something I am not yet, but which His love is trying to make me. But by that secret name God calls me. Between God and his children there are tender intimacies into which no one else can really enter.

This experience that is so intimate person is also, in a deep sense, incommunicable. This new name no one knoweth, but he that receiveth it. No one can quite tell to another all that she is finding in God. In the deepest intimacies of the soul it must ever be "My Secret to Myself." What God is to those who find Him no tongue or pen can tell. But they can speak only in stammered tones with only a hint at what they have seen.

HEAVEN

Heaven is still the same as it was in the time of the forefathers and down through centuries Heaven doesn't change for it is eternal. The heavens declare the Glory of God. It is by focussing on the things above that the mind is renewed. The creator of those heavenly bodies can also create within the creatures the brightness, calmness, steadfastness and confidence that individuals need today.

In Psychology the Höffding step – (In the terminology of Gestalt Psychology the mental step through which the perception of an image makes contact with a memory trace.) Thus if one see the "sky" and then think "cloud" the sight of the "sky" does not trigger the associated memory of "cloud" directly. There is an additional step necessary, the step whereby the stimulus "sky" contacts the memory trace to "sky" which then contacts the memory "cloud". Although the need for the Höffding step has been recognized for nearly a century it has only become regarded as important for theories of pattern perception and pattern recognition in recent years. Using such information it will become clear that as individual look towards the heavens their mind would focus on heavenly things and the stars the moon and firmament will declare what glory God has prepared for his children.

The mental steps of the Christian will be enlightened. Their focus will be on heavenly things, not on this earth. Their peception will change and thus their mind will be uplifted to the joys that is layed up in heaven when with the redeemed they will walk on streets paved with gold. The darkness will flee, there will be no more death, neither pain or sorrow. No more crying and no more sickness and sin. Heaven is the road to place their contact with the Saviour.

In the begining, when God created the heavens and the earth, so the opening chapter of genesis tell us, he separated the waters of the great deep of chaos, and placed the earth like a bubble between them. Now chaos returns and the waters of the deep crash back to reclaim the fragile island of creation. Its a picture of the results of sin. Those who have abandoned God find that all which ultimately remains is chaos and destruct. But for the few who have stuck with the creator there is safety and a place of refuge. God himself closes the door that shuts out the forces of destrustion.

The powerful image of the ark has struck a chord. It is behind Mattew's picture of the disciples finding safety from the storm in a boat with Jesus (Matthew 14:32). Peter likens baptism to rescue from the waters of chaos into the ark of the people of God (1 Peter 3:20) Nowadays many Christians are uncomfortable with the image of God of the church as a refuge. It is seen as admitting the charge that religion is escapism or a crutch for those who cannot cope with the world. There are several answers to that. I for one do not mind admitting that I can't cope alone, and that God gives me strength and hope. The world, as it is, is well worth escaping from, at least for a time And that is the second point. Noah was safe from the flood, but he emerged to start the world again. As Christian we also find refuge in God and his worship, but we emerge strengthened to serve him in the world.

Finally, the escape is not just from the pressures of the world, but from a life lived without God, which is, in the end, no life at all.

ROAD

The dust of the road comes upon us day by day. In this world, where there is so much to hide. God from us, it is so easy for the remembrance of His presence to grow dim. In the pressure of daily life, vexed and hurt by trifles, it is so easy to lose our inward peace. Living in the world, it is so easy to find ourselves thinking the world's thoughts, accepting the world's standards. The contagion of the world's slow stain passes upon us, before we are aware. So the dust of the road is upon our feet. And sometimes our feet are, splashed and soiled by the world's mine. We fall into sin. We, who said we belonged to Christ (Christian), do things altogether unworthy of Him, altogether inconsistent with our loyalty to Him. And then, soiled and dusty travellers, we have to come back to Him. And He is so gracious and understanding, so slow to blame, so ready to forgive. He is like a kindly host who bring water for his friends, that they may wash and refresh themselves.

Indeed, He Himself, as once in Jerusalem, will gird Himself with the towel and pour out the water and wash our travel – stains away and sometimes more than that. Sometimes this loving Lord will give us, unworthy as we are, the kiss of welcome, and the anointing oil with which He proclaims us honoured and well-beloved guests.

So we learn to come home to Him, after each day's confusion, toil and din, ??? loud resonant and annoying noise. A din is to force (information) into a person by continually repeating it., after the dust and heat of each days journey, to be pardoned and cleansed, our weariness refreshed, our travel – stains washed away. Till the day when, life's journey at last over, we shall commit our souls into His hands, the hands of a most merciful saviour, praying that whatever stains have come upon us in this earthly life may be washed away in the same forgiving love, and that we may be graciously admitted to sit down with Him at His table in our father's kingdom.

A person bathed and clean, coming in from the dusty road, does not need to bathe again, they only need to wash from their feet the dust of the road. And so, for the soul whom Christ has made clean, there remains the need of a daily renewal of cleansing, by which the travel-stain of the day shall be washed away. Help us to walk unstained and undisturbed even in the dust and tumult of life's busy road. The Christian on the road to the heavenly kingdom will meet many obstacles. Thus the need to be clothed in ones right mind is of absolute importance. The Psychological perspective calls for having the mind of Christ.

To be like Christ we need to understand how the mind works. Thus "at some deep level we dearly love and cherish it and see behind its surface great potential but, because of our own inadequacies, we continuously abuse it, harshly and abruptly pummelling it for imagined excess and occasionally even lock it away in some dark closet where we cannot hear its insistent whines". The mind is often seen as a separate entity and apart from the physical body. Thus when we speak of having the mind of Christ we think of the mental powers that enabled Christ to stand up and speak to the evil one with divine zeal and power. Thus the focus is typically on the effectiveness of the Word of God. When the mind as a collection of processes are viewed from a spiritual perspective the perception and cognition of the individual will be changed. Faith, hope, love, joy, peace and great contentment will be seen. Self will no longer be first, but as Christ we will see the need to put others first.

To become familiar with how the mind works it is important to know that "Reading" not of minds, but of subtle facial and muscular cues and interpreting such factors as tone of voice, manner of speaking, and other pieces of information communicated unconsciously by the one whose "mind" is being "read" can help us to become better aware of what Christ wants us to be.

Let us take a look at the life of Christ and the way he spoke, his tone of voice and other pieces of information given to us in the Word of God (the Scriptures) In the begining of God spoke and everything came into existance that was good. The manner of speech was in relation to the spirits moving upon the face of the earth, directing every action and though of Christ. When he was tempted as we are, the voice spoke words from the scriptures. When abused, hashly treated or condemned to die, it was still the use of the Word of God.

As Christians on the road to heaven we need to get inspiration from the word of God to carry us on this earthly journey of life. Thus when we read the Word of God our minds will be enlightened and our way of life will be a reflection of Christ to meet the trials and tribulations before us we need to gather -----

INSPIRATION from the Word of God. Thus when we read stories such as Job, Elijah, Samuel, Uriah and Solomon. The journey on the Christian road becomes meaningful.

Remember Job, he was a perfect and upright fearing God and staying away from evil. He had 10 children. 7 boy & 3 girls. He was rich in this world goods and was on of the richest in the Eastern countries.

When ever his children had a party or was felt to over do in their behavior it was Job who thought it was best to ask God forgiveness on their behalf.

It is amazing when the mind is fixed on things above that the evil one often comes in like a flood to try, and make a disaster of everything and everyone. In the book of Job 1:7 it is told that (Satan answered the Lord and said, from going to and fro in the earth, and from walking up and down in it.) Such is the deception of the evil one. He is constantly on the prowl! Yet with all the deception, there was something about job that even Satan could not understand. The evil one had only suspicion about Job's mind. That is Satan felt that Job's sincerity was because God had blessed him and made a hedge about him and his family.

The truth of the matter is that there was a man who feared God and kept away from evil. Yet the evil one was determined to have a confrontation with God to show that his servant job only showed appreciation to God for his material blessings. Such was the mind of an evil person, thinking that once those things were taken away, then the real Job would stand up. But the hash reality is that even when the so call things were taken. The evil one tried to hurt his flesh with sores forgetting that the Lord told him in verse 12 not to touch Job. "Only upon himself put not forth thine hand."

Having the mind of Christ was the inspiration Job showed in what he did next. When everything and everyone failed and disappeared from him. Job arose and rent his clothes. He shaved his head and fell down on the grown and worshipped. What a way to keep the mind fixed on heavenly things.

Job knew that he was born naked and was not in the least bothered that he was to returned to the earth that way. He refused to sin, but continued to bless the name of the Lord.

Elijah's is another inspiration to us today. Without sacrificing principles Elijah showed the confidence Christians can have as they enter the fire of affliction, especially in the end. 1 Kings 17:1-24 clearly gives us an insight on obedience to the voice of God. It was important that as Christians we depend on God to provide our daily bread. Wether it be bread and fish in the morning and evening with plenty of water. We must obey the voice of God. On our travels we would meet the single individual who might be struggling to make ends meet to feed her household. Yet asking them for our help should not deter us from bringing joy into their lives.

When you believe your situation is bad, then think again. Elijah was hungry and he was a minister what about the widow woman? Verse 12 said she was going to prepare her last meal and "eat it and die.

When things seems irreverable there is always a reversable end. Those we forget that helped us are the ones who never forget us. Even if situations makes us feel like giving up. We need to do like Elijah and call on the name of the Lord.

Our journey on the road can be like Elijah helping other to declare that by what we have done can only have been accomplished by God and "that the word of the Lord in thy mouth is truth." Verse 24.

Samuel heard the voice of God speaking and had to do some listening. Often we gather the inspiration to go forward by just listening to what the Lord has to say to us. In 1 Samuel 3:4-21 we see that sometime in our deep sleep we can hear the voice of the Lord speaking to us. Are we willing like Samuel to answer or are we afraid to allow God to use us in these last days. We can say "speak Lord, for thy servant heareth. Verse 9. "Although hearing includes the perception of sound primarily through the ear, a multitude of problems one would almost ensure oneself a nobel prize upon the presentation of an adequate theory of hearing that could explain satisfactorily no more than the perception of pitch and loudness. There are several candidates two major ones and several minor. The two most viable are: place theory and periodicity theory. Place theory (also known variously as resonance, hasp and piano theory) originated with the great Helmholtz in the 1860

It assumes that the perceived pitch of a tone is determined by the place of maximum vibration of the basilar membrane, the portion near the oval window being tuned for high-frequency tones, the far end near the apex of the cochlea for low-frequency tones.

"Loudness and tonal discriminability are assumed to be determined by the number of neurons activated by incoming stimulus." In general no one theory seems adequate; hearing is very complex. Therefore as Samuel we need to spend time with God and listen to his voice. Uriah heard the voice of the Lord, but sometimes as Christians we forget what we heard and try to do what we decide is best often when others try to hurt us we may have folks steal from us or even try to lead us in dangerous situations. But even when we are told to do wrong, with God's help we will survive their underminding us. Read 2 Sam 11:1-27 and you would understand why to live for Christ is better than doing that which is evil.

Even though death might come to some of us. We can still gain inspiration from Uriah and catch a glimpse of what the wisest man Solomon said in Ecclesiastes 11:8. "But if a man live many years, and rejoice in them all; yet let him remember the days of darkness; for they shall be many. All that cometh is vanity. The only way for the Christian is to learn to pray. Jesus said in (Matt 6:34.) Take therefore no thought for the tomorrow shall take thought for the things of itself of sufficient unto the the day is the evil thereof.

The Lord knows about the circumstances each of us face. He will never allow us to be tempted beyond what we can endure (1 Cor 10:13) Neither will God allow us to be overcome by events. As Christians on this journey of life, the Lord will ensure that we will have enough to cope with on each day. If we try to take tomorrow's burden on ourselves as well as today's load, we will become overburdened and we will feel that we cannot cope. When we try to deal with today, tomorrow and the possible problems of the future all at once! We as Christians are not ordering our life the way Jesus tells us. Many of us disobey what God says, and then blame God for the consequences. But when we obey God we will find that the enabling, sustaining and caring power will not allow us to fall on our Christian journey as we travel to victory in Jesus!

SPIRIT

John 14:26 states. But the conforter which is the Holy Spirit, whom the father will send in my name, he will teach you all things and bring back to your rememberance whatsoever I have said unto you. John 16:13 says that "howbeit when he, the Spirit of truth, is come, he will guide you into all truth: for he shall not speak of himself; but whatsoever he shall hear, that shall he speak: and he will shew you things to come."

For the outpouring of the Spirit every person of the cause of truth should pray. The spirit can never be poured out when there is confusion and hated towards others. When people stop speaking evil and thinking of ways to destroy others, then the workings of the Holy Spirit will be seen in their lives. In Acts 2:1-12 it is shown how when people are of one accord in one place the spirit will come from heaven suddenly as a rushing mighty wind. We need to understand that the people were seated and the spirit appeared to them as cloven tongues of fire. The results were seen in the words they spoke.

People from every country and of different nationality were able to understand what was been said. Thus they were shocked to know that these were people from the same church.

There would alway be sceptics that would cast doubt on the wonderful works of God. For when they behold the working of the spirit, they will find excuses to say that people had some form of alcoholic drink. You see, once the spirit is working within the life of the individual. There is no place or language the person is not affraid to stand up and be heard.

These are the days in which the spirit will be poured out (verse 17) and everyone including women, men, young and old will see visions and dream dreams. The signs and wonders we see today are a reminder of whether we want to be saved in Gods kingdom or be lost. The spirit helps in the santification of our lives and gives us power to share the message of truth to others. Thus the work of God will be finished and the day will come when the Lord will fulfill his promise and return for those who have walked the Christian journey in spirit and truth.

The well-known conversation between Jesus and Nicodemus, the prominent Christian who came to see Jesus secretly by night is actually about the two worlds we live in (John 3:3-6) One of the "flesh" and the "spirit". Nicodemus's flattering greeting, was met by what seems to be a bald statement by Jesus: "You must be born from above" or be "born anew". The conversation as it develops centres around this insistence of Jesus: people are both flesh and spirit, and human life was incomplete without the element of spirit.

We as Christians have to be born of "water and spirit" (the capital letter "s" is a tricky one in this passage!) presumably the "water" here is the water of physical birth. I can think of the astonishment moles have when they hear of their wives or mother's talking about "water breaking" before birth, but having no idea how much water there would be. We are all "born of water", but as we travel this Christian journey, we also need to be "born of the Spirit." Without the spiritual element in our lives we are, in the teaching of Jesus, only half human. That is the way we were made "in the image of God". So to concentrate in child development on the physical, intellectual and emotional growth but neglect the spiritual is to deprive the child of its human birthright "you must be born from above". Thus as the psychology of Christianity gives reflection, we in this word put so much emphasis on education, health and mental stability but where does the life of the spirit comes in? Are we in danger of getting our values distorted. Remember we are the light of the world, a city on a hill cannot be hid. The light of our souls shines, but a brighter light shines over a wider range, and a dimmer light shines on a smaller range. The extent to which our light shines is the width and depth and breadth and light of our spiritual connection with Christ's truth.

TRUST

Everyone was born with a gift, not to be used, but to be used by God. There is a sacred agreement to accomplish specific goals. We have a committment in fulfulling our being. That is why when we succeed in accomplishing our goals, in fulfilling our responsibilities, there is a richness and a specialness to the soul spiritual awareness. We all have a task to do. It may be the task of raising a family, or communicating ideas through writing. When the deepest part of you becomes engaged in what you are doing, when four activities and actions become gratifying and purposeful, when what you do serves both yourself and others, when you do not tire within but seek the sweet satisfaction of your life and your work, you are doing what you were meant to be doing. When the spirit of truth comes you will be offered light. There will be encouragement in each moment to your fullest growth and development, yet you cannot be prevented from your learning or your growing or your moving through your Christian experiences and letting your experiences influence you. This is so even if you are able to communicate with the Holy Spirit.

Your experiences will move you right or left, and you will ask the Holy Spirit this question or that. If you move left, your question will be entirely different than if you had moved right, and the reality that you open by that question will be entirely different. Listening to the spirits and moving as the spirit directs you, becomes a partnership of challenging you to come to terms with the full width and breadth and depth of your soul's responsible choice. It is not that you give permission to be mindlessly manipulated. It is that you give permission to be shown the fullest of your power and guided to its use. Let go of what you think is just reward. Let go trust. Be who you are. The rest is up to the Holy Spirit. Take your hands off the steering wheel. Be able to say to God, "thy will be done", and to know it within your soul. Spend time in this thought. Consider what it means to say. "Thy will be done". And allow your life to go into the hands of God completely. The final piece of the Christian journey is letting go and let God take control. From creation we were guided by unseen hands, this guidance happened nontheless in its perfection and in its balance. That is what will happen now, when we put our trust in God, knowing that the heavens declear the Glory of God. We as Christians must be reminded that we are supported and are not going it alone upon this earth. When you ask for guidance and assistance, simply assume that it immediately is pouring forward you may need to work a while to relax your mind into receptivity, or you may need to have lunch or do whatever it is that you need to do in order to relax your mind to hear or to feel, but live in the total assumption that the moment that you ask for guidance it is pouring in. Trusting means that the circumstance that you are in is working toward your best and most appropriate end. There is no when to that. There is no if to that. It is let go and trust God He will provide, and so it shall be let go of all. Allow yourself to pray.

Prayer is moving into a personal relationship with God. Thus it is impossible to have a thought that is a secret for God hears our prayer. When we pray along our Christian journey, we draw to God and each other. Prayer brings grace and grace calms us. Grace is the tranquilizer of the soul. With grace comes a knowing that we are experiencing what is necessary for our journey. It calms our sense of knowing. Live in the trust that when it is appropriate, every little piece will fall into place and we will see clearly the way forward in our journey through life.

Trust allows you to give. Giving is abundant. As you give so shall be given to you. If you give with judgment, limitation and stinginess, that is what you will create in your life. Don't forget, what you do to others is what you get done to you on this Christian journey. If you radiate love, you recieved it. If fear and suspicion that is what you are asking for. Thus when you trust you allow for a blissfull experience, so you can laugh at the richness and beauty and playfulness of the created life on the earth. The path the Christian walk now is not unknown to God. The pains and distresses and violences that we experience can be considered as signposts along the path that we have chosen. We as Christians on the journey can also rely on the Word of God, thus we can glean from Scriptures

19/04/05

used in work NI
25/05/05

REMEMBER THE TSUNAMI?

I can remember that dark night when a sudden storm swept over the Asian Pacific. This to me was an example of the storms that attempted to destroy my Christian experiences (2001-2005) I was being tossed about on the raging seas of strife, the howling winds and angry waves seems to come from all directions causing me to fear that all hope of surviving as a Christian was gone. Throughout nights I rode in the teeth of the pale of strife. The surface of the troubles was like a boiling caldron, and its frothing billows tossed my life like an autumn leaf. After many years and months, days, hours of hard thinking and watchfulness, in the gleam of the darkness, looking closely at the Word of God, I cried out to God (Matthew 14:26; Mark 6:49) above the roar of the raging situations. It was during those dark nights that I heard the assuring words, "Be of Good Cheer. It is I: be not afraid". The moment Jesus took over my life, the winds quieted and I become calm, such is the Christian experiences.

What is TRUTH?

John 17:17 speaks of God's word as truth. "In logic, a characteristic of a proposition which follows logically from the axioms in use and previous proposition whose truth is known as well as a characteristic of a proposition, statement or belief which corresponds with "reality as it is known is truth."

As Christians that which is true can only be from a higher source from ourselves, and must be shown to be true when put to the test. Such truths are found from the Word of God. Thus the life of Christ and the world is truth.

Without Christ the existance of the word and all that is there in would not speak of truth. Truth began with God and ends with God. The Word was God and the Word is God, therefore if the Word of God is truth. We as Christians need to seek after truth every day of our lives. For the Word of the Lord is right; and all his works are done in truth (Ps. 33:4). God's mercy is great unto the heavens and his truth is unto the clouds (Ps 57:10) It was Christ mercy and truth that met together: and righteousness and peace that have kissed each other.

(Ps 85:10) Thus as Christian the mercy extented to us while we were yet sinners gives us the reassurance that the truth of Gods words are sure. We as Christians have a more sure word of prophesy whereby we can know the truth and be set free from the quilt and sinning.

Truth as we know only comes from fortifying our minds with the Word of God. The lessons we obtain therein gives us the wisdom, knowledge and understanding to meet the challenges we face in our daily lives. Such lessons of truth as seen in the gospels, tell us that that our salvation has been assured through Jesus and his death on Calvary. It was the old rugged cross that made the difference for the Christians. Truth came down to earth and made the difference. Thus we as Christians have nothing to fear as long as we hold on to the truth as is found in the Word of God. It is only by studding the Word of God can the Christian come to behold the lessons from the life of Christ that make them wise unto salvation and gain the insight needed to walk the Christian pathway.

Insight

Such great insights can be obtained from the story of Joseph. In Enid Blyton tales from the Bible 1947 Fourth Edition Methuen & Co. Ltd London. The story is told of the boy with the coloured coat, the unkind brothers, the slave - boy Joseph, the king's strange dreams, Joseph and his brothers.

Joseph father had 10 sons who helped him in the work of guarding and tending the cattle and sheep. Sometimes in our everyday experiences as Christians. There always seem to be one child or sometimes two who are favored more by our father or mother. Such insight can be gleaned from Jacob, as he had loved Joseph and Benjamin above all the others. They were the two youngest. Joseph was a strong youth, but Benjamin was only a small child. Joseph loved him and played with him when he had time. Joseph was loved by his father and spoke of him lovingly, and gave him many presents.

(Genesis 37-1-36)

When we speak of insight, we as Christians need to know that there is an ability to perceive and understand

"Oxford Dictionary" the true nature of something." Thus when we observe that the elder brothers becoming jealous of Joseph and hated him, all but the eldest, Ruben, who like him. The cruel words spoken to him by his other brothers and their unfriendliness towards him all began to happen when he got that wonderful coat, bright as a rainbow in its many colours.

There are several more specialized meaning of insight. This can be to personal insight, where the standard parlance, any self-awareness, self-knowledge or self-understanding becomes meaningful. Note that there are distinctions made between intellectual insight, which is a kind of theoretical understanding of one's condition or of the underlying psychodynamics of one's actions but still leaves one alienated from the self and emotional insight, which is regarded as true deep understanding.

When Joseph brothers saw him in the coat, they hated to see him wearing it, and they scorned him and spoke spitefully to him.

Joseph brothers also disliked him too, about the strange dreams that he had. They said he always had queer dreams, dreams so vivid that they seemed quite real to him.

Two additional meaning relate to situational or environmentally stimulated insights. One is the novel, clear, compelling apprehension of the truth of something occuring without overt recourse to memories or past experiences and the other within gestalt psychology, the process by which problems are solved. In this sense, insight characterizes a sudden reorganization or restructuring of the pattern or significance of events allowing one to grasp relationships relevant to the solution. Here insight represents a kind of learning and is characterized in an all-or-none fashion".

Maybe Joseph dreams had meaning said his brother Ruben. The unkindness of his brothers were the begining of the end of his dreams. Yet when his father sent him to seek out his brothers. They devised ways and means to kill him. They took hold of him roughly. They stripped off his coat of many colours. They bound him hand and foot and threw him into a pit, rolling a big stone over the mouth. Then they went to find the presents Joseph had brough and were soon sitting down eating the food and drinking the wine he brought for them.

As Christians evethough nine brothers sat eating, the company do get greater when others pass by or join in. You see the men coming towards Joseph's brothers were traders and sometimes to trade seems much easier at times than to do what is right. They were fierce men, trading over the desert travelling great distances on their camels. They took spicery and balm and myrrh, sweet-smelling and rare, down the desert tracks into Egypt, and brought back with them cotton and silk. Sometimes, too, they bought and sold children as slaves.

When the nine brothers saw these desert traders on their camel coming they had an idea. One brother said not to kill Joseph but to get rid of him and tell their father a lie. So off they went and dragged Joseph out of the pit and unbound him while he was still dazed and shocked. Joseph was sold to the traders and looked around to see his brothers walking away in the distance. Dipping Joseph coat in the blood of an animal, they took the blood-stained coat in sorrow and dispair to their father to prove that Joseph was dead.

Whilst Jacob was so bitterly weeping for Joseph whom he thought dead, Joseph was being taken to Egypt. On his arrival he was bought by Potiphar, a rich Egyptian and an officer of Pharaoh, the King of Egypt. Sometimes as Christians on the road to the heaven kingdom, we find ourselves in strange places. Joseph was in a strange place, but soon learnt every inch of Potiphar's house and garden, and because of his keen mind soon understood how to run the place. When those around Joseph saw that his lifestyle was different, he was soon put in charge of Potiphar's household. So when his master was away Joseph saw to everything.

Doing the best we can in difficult situations can cause the evil one to unleash poinsonous venom against us. People like Potiphar's wife often dislike us and will speak evil about us. You see Joseph had fled Potiphar's wife advances, and she was furious. This led to a confrontation with Potiphar who believed the lie his wife had told. Thus Joseph was thrown into prison.

But, even in prison, Joseph remained honest and true. Even the governor of the prison trusted Joseph and soon put him in charge of all the prisioners. As

Christian the choices we make when shut up in dark situations of life, often have consequential results. Friends we meet and friend we make can be a blessing or a cure to us. Joseph was able to listen and interpret the dreams of those ground him as well as the king's dream. Pharaoh listened and marvelled at the good sense and wisdom of Joseph. He was amazed at the way Joseph had explained his dreams.

While Joseph became the governor of Egypt, his father and brothers were starving in their homeland. You see sometimes as Christians the time of famine can be a time of repentance and healing. Joseph helped his family eventhough they did not deserve to be helped. The test of their honesty and integrity meant that the way they lived in the past could be an indication of their present state of mind. But as Joseph saw in their behaviours and attitude an indication of change from within. Joseph took his father to Pharoah, and then he gave his father's family the fair land of Goshen, where they were able to live happily together. His family were looked after by him whilst the years of famine lasted, when they were over, the family of Jacob remained in Egypt, where their children grew up in great numbers becoming rich and powerful men.

They were happy there, although they were strangers to the country with different customs, and worshipped a God whom the Egyptians did not know. Thus as Christians the need to accept the challenges that we face can often become the stepping stone of our rejoicing.

ACCEPTANCE

The acceptance of the will of God for the Christian must be seen in the way we focus on those thing that are meaningful to us. Thus when we understand Psalm 19:1-14 we can clearly see that the "Heaven declare the glory of God: and the firmament sheweth his handiwork. Day unto day uttereth speech, and night unto night sheweth knowledge. There is no speech or language where their voice is not heard. Their line is gone out through all the earth, and their words to the end of the world. In them hath he set a tabernacle for the sun. Which is as a bridegroom coming out of his chamber and rejoiceth as a strong man to run a race. His going forth is from the end of the heaven, and circuit unto the ends of it: and there is nothing hid from the heat thereof. The law of the Lord is perfect, converting the soul: the testimony of the Lord is sure, making wise the simple. The statues of the Lord are right, rejoicing the heart the commandment of the Lord is pure, enlightening the eyes. The fear of the Lord is clean, enduring for ever: the judgements of the Lord are true and righteous altogether. More to be desired are they than gold, yea, than much fine gold sweeter also than honey and the honeycomb. Moreover by them is thy servant warned: and in keeping of them there is great reward. Who can understand his errors? Cleanse thou me from secret faults. Keep back thy servant also from presumptuous sins: let them not have dominion over me: then shall I be upright, and I shall be innocent from the great transgression.

Let the words of my mouth, and the meditation of my heart, be acceptable in thy sight, O Lord. My strength and my redeemer. As Christians the things we see, hear and say shall help us to understand the needs of others.

NEED

Christians have the need for love, Cathexis, achievement, affiliation and tissue. This need can be some thing or some state of affairs which, if present, would improve the wellbeing of the person. A need, in this sense, may be something basic and biological (food) or it may involve social and personal factors and derive from complex forms of learning (achievement, prestige).

Another form of need which is of great importance for the child of God can only be the longing for an internal state that is in need of the things or state of affairs which makes one wise to spiritual things. The need for love can be summed up for the Christian in 1 Cor 13:1-13. It tells us that eventhough we may be able to speak well and have high sounding tones and intonation or can be able to solve many of todays problems. Without love it is a waste of time. There can be some of us who have all the faith to remove the obstacles in our pathway. While having the ability to feed those that are hungry or destitute. But without love it profiteth them nothing.

Christian must understand that on the journey their love must suffer long, and be kind. There love must not be envieous never be proud or rash. The love they show must reflect the love of God. They cannot be provoked or think evil of others. Never should the Christian rejoice when others do wrong, but be willing to rejoice when the truth is told. As Christians we need to learn how to bear all things as well as believe all things as we hope and endure the moments of waiting for our Lords return.

Since love will never fail us and all around will come to an end. It is time that what me know now in past will soon be done away with, and those childest thoughts and attitudes we once posess. Let us leave them behind us and become grown ups desiring the sincere milk of the Word of God

For now we can only see things through a glass darkly, but when we behold the saviour face we will understand the faith, hope and love that endureth forever. The cathexis need will then be observed when we convey the love to others when we see them struggling on the journey of life. Thus we as Christians will strive for the need of achievement as characterized by D. C. McClelland and J. W. Atkinson, the desire to compete with a standard of excellence. It is treated as a socially characterized need with two critical components: a set of internatized standards that represent personal achievement or fullfillment, and a theoretical energizing or motivating condition that impels us towards attempts to meet these standards.

Once we as Christians come to understand the will of God for our lives. The need for affiliation in H. Murray term for the need to be with other people, to socialize form friendship and cooperate with other will become reality for each Christian individual.

INDIVIDUAL

Individual psychology has been historically used in the term roughly synonymously with what is now called differential psychology. Today it is associated with the personality theory of Alfred Adler (1870-1937) The primary concept is that of inferiority and the crux of the human condition is assumed to be the struggle against feelings of inferiority be they conscious or unconscious, physical, psychological or social.

As Christians we struggle to become like Christ. Yet we are told that in all our Christian endeavours we are to obey Gods words not while others are presence but now much more in the absence of other. We are to work out our own salvation with fear and trembling". (Philippians 2:12). We have to allow our physical minds and body to be united to Christ. Thus we are to eat, sleep, work and play with all the strenght that the Lord have given to us. Our bodies should be furnished with the right food to keep our minds focus on Christ. Anything that will hinder the physical body should be put away.

Late hours of nighty pleasures, diets consisting of unhealthy produc??? worship of other Gods and doing that which is consciously and unconsciously wrong. "Flee fornication. Every sin that a person doeth is without the body: but he that committeth fornication sinneth against his own body. What? Know ye not that your body is the temple of the Holy Ghost which is in you, which ye have of God, and ye are not your own? For ye are bought with a price. Therefore glorify God in your body, and in your spirit, which are God's. 1 Cor 6:18-20)

Taking care of the individual self should also make us understand the psychological self which is one of the more dominant aspects of human experience. This is the compelling sense of one's unique existence, what philosophers have traditionally called the issue of personal identity or of the self. Accordingly, this term finds itself rather well represented in psychological theory, particularly in areas of social and developmental psychology, the study of personality and the field of psychopthology.

As we come close to God, we will begin to see what plans there is for each of us as we continue on this Christian pathway. We will lay all our daily plan at God feet, and daily commune with the saviour. Our thought, actions and motivation will be towards God's will and what we do or say will reflect our close connection with Christ.

The love of Christ will constrain us. And the joy of serving in whatever avenue of this life will bring out the best in each of us. Whatever we find our hands doing, we would do with all our might and when our days are dreary or sad we can still find comfort in knowing that all things work together for our good. In our journey we will know that

"Whatsoever things are true,
Whatsoever things are honest,
Whatsoever things are just,
Whatsoever things are pure,
Whatsoever things are lovely,
Whatsoever things are of a good report: If there be any virture and if there me any praise, think on these things.

THINK

To be aware of what the Christian think can be related to the life they lead. Thinking most generally means "any covert cognitive or mental manipulation of ideas, images, symbols, words, propositions, memories, concepts, precepts, beliefs or intentions. In short when we think it encompasses "all of the mental activities associated with concept-formation, problem-solving, intellectual functioning, creativity, complex learning, memory symbolic processing and imagery.

Few term in Psychology cast such as broad net and few encompass such as rich array of connotations and entailments. But certain components nonetheless lie at the core of all the usages of thinking. When we as Christians begin to think of those things that makes us happy. Such thinking is treated as a covert or implicit process that is not directly observable. The existence of a though process is inferred either from what I have written or by observing the behavioral acts of those mentioned in these writings. As we begin to think on what is written, we can generally assume that there was some manipulation of some "elements of thought" was involved thinking that converged on the scriptures is characterized by bringing together or synthesizing the information and knowledge focused on a solution to the Christian journey such thinking is often associated with problem-solving, particularly with problems that relates to "the Psychology of Christianity."

These admonitions can only be seen in a critical way of thinking when we allow a cognitive strategy consisting largely of continual checking and testing of the bibical truths outlined. Thus we will find possible solutions to guide us in what we do or say. Critical thinking therefore should enable us as Christians to find new insights into the Word of God and seek solutions that will help us to think in a divergent manner. Thus our thinking will be characterized by a process of "moving away" from paths that lead us to destruction. We will have a diverging of ideas to encompass a variety of relevant aspects of our lives. Such thinking will be associated with our creativity and we will then be able to yield our minds to Christ and find new joy serving the Lord while we await his return.

YIELD

Romans 6:13
Romans 6:19
I speak after the manner of men because of the infirmity of your flesh: for as ye have yielded your members servants to uncleanness and to iniquity unto iniquity: even so now yield your members servants to righteousness unto holiness. Neither yield ye your members as instruments of unrighteousness unto sin: but yield yourselves unto God, as those that are alive from the dead, and your members as instruments of righteousness unto God. For to be carnally minded is death; but to be spiritually minded is life and peace. (Romans 8: 6, 18 25, 26, 28, 31, 35, 37-39.) For I reckon that the sufferings of this present time are not worthy to be compared with the glory which shall be revealed in us. But if we hope for that we see not, then do we with patience wait for it. Likewise the spirit also helpeth our infirmities. For we know not what we should pray for as we ought: but the spirit itself maketh intercession for us with groanings which cannot be uttered

Yet as Christians we know that all things work together for good to them that love God, to them who are the called according to his purpose. What shall we then say to these things? If God be for us, who can be against us? Even so who shall separate us from the love of Christ? Shall tribulation, or distress, or persecution, or famine, or nakedness, or peril or sword? Nay in all these things we are more than conquerors through him that loved us.

I am persuaded that neither death, or life, nor angels, nor principalities, nor powers, nor things present, nor things to come. Nor height, nor depth, nor any other creature, shall be able to separate us from the love of God, which is in Christ Jesus our Lord. This work is according to Romans 9:1-3 I say the truth in Christ, I lie not, my conscience also bearing me witness in the Holy Ghost. That I have great heaviness and continual sorrow in my heart. For I could wish that myself were separated from Christ for my brethren, my family according to the flesh. God blessed for ever. Amen.

12/01/2000

God's will is made known as readily by the flight of a dove as by the words of a prophet, or as much by the everyday circumstances of our lives as by an exalted experience of prayer or worship.

Matt 18:21-22 2/2/2000

Jesus, in the New Testament gave a further explanation why we have to forgive those that wrong us without pre-conditions. It was Peter who asked Jesus how often he would be obliged to forgive a brother that continuous wrongs him. Should he be forgiven up to seven times? Now you may wonder why Peter specifies the number of time as seven. The answer is, that Peter, just the same as Jesus, was a pious Jew. In Judiasm as well as in Christianity seven was thought of as a holy number. There are seven day of the creation, seven spirits before the throne of God, seven days in the week, seven graces, seven divisions in the Lord's prayer, seven ages of man there are seven phases of the moon, every seventh year was sabbatical, and the seven times seven years was the jubilee. The three great Jewish feasts lasted seven days, and between the first and the second of these feast were seven weeks. Levitical purification lasted seven days. We have seven church of Asia, seven candlesticks, seven stars, seven trumpets, seven horns, and there were ten times seven elders. Ten times seven Isralites went to Egypt, the exile lasted the same number of years, ect. The number seven is frequently used to signify a long time, a great many times, or indefinitely. So when Peter asks, if he should forgive as often as seven times, he means not exactly seven times, but a great many times. In the same way it can be interpreted as a long period of time with a definite ending, which of course means that there is a limit to how often, for how long and up to which gravity one should forgive.

Jesus recognized the openness of interpretation of this question at once and decided to clarify this point once and for all, still using the same figure of speech as Peter: "I do not say seven times; I say seventy times seven". From the customs of the Old Testament, the Jewish law, that a God-fearing man had to forgive a brother for all the sins he had committed against him at least once every year, it follows that if Peter was to take the figure that Jesus had given him literally, he would have had to continue to pardon those that had wronged him for 490 years, longer than any man's life. In other words Jesus told him that forgiveness must be unrestricted by time and number, indefinite and everlasting, in Jewish terms that means even after death.

25/2/2000

PRAYER is not an occasional resource for hours of need, no is it the luxury of rare and beautiful moments. Prayer is a duty I owe to God, an offering of love and devotion that I must bring to Him. Day by day there are mercies for which I ought to thank Him sins for which I need His forgiveness, plans and purposes that I must bring before the master of my life, friends whose need. I must commend to Him. And so not only should I have my appointed time of prayer; it is good for me to have some method of prayer, some ordered routine of petition, thanksgiving, intercession, so that when no special impulse leads me to some special prayer, my heart may turn aside at the appointed time, tread obediently the accustomed path to prayer.

So I come to learn one of life's greatest lessons – that every event of my passing day is an indication of God's will for me. The one thing needful for my soul is not even that I should have adequate time for prayer; it is that I should do God's will, as moment by moment that will unfolds itself before me. Sometimes He wills for me the quiet of prayer, and sometimes the pressure of busy life. Today God may will that I should rest in His presence, listening to His voice and rejoicing in His love. Tomorrow God my let my life be so crowded that I scarce can pause, save to remember with thankfulness that I am His. Let me accept God's will moment by moment, eager only to be where in that moment God wills me to be, asking only that I may not miss what in that moment God wills to give me.

MY PRAYER

Our Father which is in heaven, let me not miss whatever you have for me this day. Make me ready for all your perfect will, ready to understand what you want of me in every circumstance so that I can meet every situation with your help to recieve your message through whatever voice you choose to speak to me. Help me to live my life this day, eager and attentive to every leading of your will, active in your service, and yet with a quiet spirit that even in the busiest hour can be at rest in you. So may I know at once the joy of serving you and the secret of your presence through the fellowship of thy son, Jesus Christ my Lord. AMEN

31/3/2000

Whenever I am troubled and lost in deep despair, I bundle all my worries up and go to God in prayer. I tell him I am sick at heart, and lost and lonely, too that my mind is deeply burdened, and I don't know what to do. But I know he stilled the tempest, and calmed the angry sea, and I humbly ask if, in His love, He'll do the same for me. And then just keep quiet, and think only thought of peace, and in the shadow of His arm my anxious cares will cease.

18/5/2000

Deceit

(Gen 12:10-13) speaks of Abram becoming fearful of his life when he was about to enter Egypt. He said to his wife to say she was his sister because they the Egyptians would kill him to get her.

Faith is all very well, but we have to live in the real world. You've probably heard comments like that. Of course you have. In fact, if truth be told, we've almost all made them at some time. Not, perhaps, out loud, so that we can hear what we are really saying, but quietly, in our secret thoughts, stifles any actual full-blown decision but just letting ourselves follow a course that is unworthy, deceitful or cowardly

Abram had travelled through Canaan, where God has promised to give that land to his descendants. But promises are all very well when one is secure and wealthy. Famine changes all that, and, Abram must throw himself on the mercy of the Egyptians. Surely they will kill him to get his lovely wife Sarah. So he passes her off as available to be a concubine for Pharaoh (and get a good deal out of the bargain). We're not told what Sarah thought of all this. God, though, is not pleased. And neither is Pharaoh. When he finds out (by being afflicted with plagues from God) he sends Abram packing. Abram had made two mistakes. Firstly, he had allowed fear to paint the Egyptians as monsters. In fact they were not. "Why didn't you just say she was your wife?" Asked Pharaoh Abram did not say, "because fear crippled his judgement and destroyed his faith." But he could have spoken the truth.

Secondly, Abram had underestimated God. Not by failing to believe God would keep him safe. Safety is not a divine promise. He had failed to realize that the God he served demanded integrity and holiness. God is not served by lying and cheating. His demand is for truth, and the faith to know that truth will be honoured by God.

30/???/2000

The words we speak have a direct and definite effect upon our thoughts. Thoughts create words, for words are the vehicles of ideas. But words also affect thoughts and help to condition if not to create attitudes. In fact, what often passes for thinking starts with talk.

27/6/2000

The Parable of the Soil

Matthew 13:3-8: Listen! A sower went out to sow. ------ let anyone with ears listen!

This is usually called the "parable of the sower" but really its the parable of the soil. The sower in the story simply does his job. The seed of the "Word of the Kingdom" is good seed. Nothing is wrong with the "message". The determining factor in the harvest, then, is neither the sower nor the seed, but the soil. In the immortal saying from gardening programmes, "the answer lies in the soil."

That raises a problem of course. What can we do about the soil? Most of us know that in sharing the word of God with others we are called to "sow the seed." And we know that there's nothing wrong with the message. The gospel is good. The problem is in those who hear it. - the "rocky soil" that can't be penetrated, the life which is like a public footpath where nothing can take root for long, the shallow person who can offer no depth for the seed to penetrate, the life so caught up in worldly concerns that it has no time for spiritual truth. We can't change the seed, so can we change the soil? It seems to me that that is the challenge here (to prepare the ground) as a good farmer would, breaking up the stony soil, digging over the path, rooting out the seeds, and so on. By prayer and care, the soil can be changed .... but only if it wishes to be! In reflection the whole story is really about human responsibility. “Let anyone with ears listen.” The seed is good. The sower is faithful. But ears need to be opened. Let’s pray that they will be.

Mat 13:43

Printed in the United States
By Bookmasters